WALT DISNEY

Donald and His Friends

Twin Books

Tonight is a very important night for Donald Duck: it's his birthday!

He spent the whole day scrubbing and dusting and cleaning his house for the big party he is throwing for his friends. He was so tired after the hard day's work that he lay down on the sofa for a short nap, but instead he fell into a deep sleep!

Driiiing! Driiiing! The doorbell rang, but Donald
was in the middle of a dream. He thought the doorbell
was the telephone ringing. But when he reached over
in his dream to pick it up, he slipped off the sofa and
fell onto the floor.

"Ouch!" he muttered as he hit the floor. "I must
have fallen asleep!"

Driiing! Driiing! The doorbell rang again. "Oh! No!
My guests are here! I haven't cooked dinner yet!" he
thought in a panic as he went to open the door.

"Daisy! What a stroke of luck!" he said as he opened the door. "You must help me! I am running very late and…"

"Me? Help you?" laughed Daisy. "You men are all alike! What do you want me to do?"

"I need help in the kitchen. I haven't even started to cook dinner yet. I fell asleep!" Donald explained.

"Okay, I will cook dinner, but first you must tell me what you think of my new shoes," said Daisy with a smile.

"They are very elegant, Daisy…" said Donald, admiring.

"And the gift I brought you?"

"Beautiful, but it's too much," replied Donald. He was very happy to see her.

As Donald unwrapped Daisy's gift — she had given him a wonderful fly-swatter — the doorbell rang again. Minnie and Mickey had arrived. Donald led them to the living room.

"Where is Daisy?" asked Minnie. "She told us she would come early."

"Daisy? Well…she…" stammered Donald. He was too embarrassed to tell Minnie that Daisy was cooking dinner in the kitchen.

Driiing! Driiing! The doorbell again! Donald left his guests to open the door. What a surprise! Standing in the doorway was a huge present, and this present could even talk and walk!

"Happy Birthday!" it said, and Donald recognized the voice.

"Goofy!" he laughed as he undid the wrapping. "What a wonderful surprise!"

Pluto was the fourth guest to arrive. Donald's three nephews, Huey, Dewey and Louie, heard their friend bark. They ran out of the kitchen where they had been helping Daisy. They couldn't wait to play with him.

They reached for Donald's gift. But Pluto wouldn't let them have it. After all, it was Donald's birthday, not theirs.

Huey, Dewey and Louie were disappointed. But everyone started to sing 'Happy Birthday!' to Donald, and they joined the chorus. They had a good laugh. Hadn't Goofy looked funny wrapped up as a gift?

Mickey Mouse stepped forward and unwrapped his gift. "This is my gift to you," he said as he pulled a handsome top-hat out of the box. "Something you can wear to a grand ball." Donald didn't know what to say. But Daisy, who had overheard Mickey from the kitchen, popped her head out the door and said with a smile, "A grand ball, Mickey? What a wonderful idea!" Donald wasn't so sure.

"Come on, Uncle Donald! Try it on!" shouted his nephews impatiently.

"Yes, Donald, put it on!" seconded Daisy with a twinkle in her eye. "Show us how handsome you are!"

Donald obliged. As he placed the hat on his head, a stream of sparkling light and golden stars trickled out of it.

"A magician's hat! A magician's hat!" shouted the nephews. Mickey told them to quiet down.

"Listen!" he whispered. Everybody hushed. From inside the hat came a faint and faraway voice....

"Mr. Rabbit, where are you going so fast?" said the voice. Donald flipped the hat over. "Alice in Wonderland!" he exclaimed. Everybody rushed over and took a peek.

"What is she looking for?" asked Louie.

"She is after the White Rabbit!" explained Dewey.

"Will she catch him?"

"Of course she will," replied Dewey, "but only after she meets with the Cheshire Cat and the March Hare and the terrible Queen of Hearts in the kingdom of cards!"

"What a birthday this is!" said Donald, delighted.

"You haven't seen anything yet!" said Mickey, watching his friend hold his head in amazement.

The resonant sound of cymbals filled the room, and was followed by a gentle tune played on a harp.

Out of the hat came Merlin the Wizard, holding his magic wand in one hand and his wizard's cap in place with the other.

Peter Pan was next, and Huey exclaimed, "It is a good thing he didn't bring that awful Captain Hook and his crocodile with him!"

Merlin raised his magic
wand and whispered his
very ancient magical
formula:
   "Abracadabrus,
abracadabra, abracadabri,
abracadabro!"
   Immediately, a huge
present appeared.

Donald couldn't wait to open *this* present. It was huge!

Out of the box came the biggest birthday cake he had ever seen. His little nephews jumped up and down with anticipation. The whole room filled with applause.

Donald did not know how to thank Merlin for his thoughtfulness. "Don't think about thanking me now!" advised the wizard with a smile. "This is only the beginning!"

"Abracadabrus,
abracadabra, abracadabri,
abracadabro!" whispered
Merlin again. The cake
grew even larger. Then a
piece of chocolate broke off
and a door appeared!

The door opened and
Snow White and the Seven
Dwarfs stepped out. Each
greeted Donald with a
present.

Before Donald could finish thanking his unexpected guests, the cake grew again. It took the shape of a magical castle. Its walls were made of caramel and its towers of chocolate. "It's Cinderella's castle!" exclaimed one of the guests.

Cinderella came forward and offered Donald a pumpkin. "She's making fun of him!" giggled Louie.

But the pumpkin turned into a sportscar when Donald put it on the floor. Huey, Dewey and Louie couldn't believe their eyes!

"Don't look so surprised!" teased Cinderella, and to Donald she said, "Come on, get behind the wheel!" Donald jumped into the car.

"Who wants to go for a ride?" he called out.

"Me!" shouted Huey.

"Me too!" yelled Dewey.

"And me too!" cried Louie, afraid he'd be left out.

Everyone went for a ride
in Donald's sportscar.
Merlin had no more tricks
up his sleeve, so Mickey
sent them back into the hat.
"Good bye, Peter Pan!"
said Louie. "Will you come
back for *my* birthday?"
"Yes, I will!" promised
Peter Pan as he disappeared
into the hat.

Driiing! Driiing! The doorbell rang.

"Who could be coming so late?" wondered Donald.

"Uncle Scrooge! I did not expect you to come," said Donald, surprised.

"He must have smelled the food," giggled Daisy.

"And he said to himself, 'I'll go and have a free dinner!'" added Minnie, laughing.

But Uncle Scrooge said instead with a sob, "I just was the victim of a robbery!"

"A robbery?" cried Donald in disbelief.

"Yes! A most horrible robbery!" insisted Uncle Scrooge. "If only I had not bought you that beautiful present!"

"What beautiful present?" asked Donald.

"The one I bought you, of course!" said Uncle Scrooge, annoyed. "I was on my way here carrying your present when a robber..."

"...jumped on top of you and ran away with my present!" finished Donald, who did not believe this tale of misery. "If you search your pocket," teased Donald, "you might find a little piece of it!"

Uncle Scrooge searched his pockets in vain. "Uncle Scrooge! You've got such bad luck!" said everyone, tongue-in-cheek.

"Since you lost my present, Uncle Scrooge, take this one!" said Donald.

Uncle Scrooge realized that they were making fun of him. He flew into a rage.

"Is this how you treat me?" he shouted. "And to think I have been so generous to you!" Everyone burst out laughing.

Uncle Scrooge was livid. He threw whatever he could get his hands on at Donald. But Donald ducked, and the presents, books, lamps, telephone hit...

… Medusa, Madam Mim, Cruella de Vil, and Maleficent! The witches had come when they heard that Merlin, Cinderella and Snow White had been invited to the party. They had hid in a dark corner of the room, but now they were discovered. So they left as fast as they could, to everyone's delight.

But the last object Uncle Scrooge hurled across the room knocked Goofy over. He was very surprised, and he worried that something else would hit him as well. But instead, a beautiful and soothing music filled the room. Even Uncle Scrooge forgot his anger and listened to the music.

"Thank you, Happy, for your cheerful music!" said Goofy, relieved. "Thank you, Bashful, for the sweet sound of your guitar! And thank you, Sneezy and Doc, for the trumpet and the cymbals!"

The Seven Dwarfs were welcomed with a round of applause.

For once, Sleepy was
wide awake, pulling an
organ on wheels, while
Grumpy was at the keyboard
in a good mood!

"Would you care to dance?" Donald asked the beautiful Snow White.

"I would love to!" replied Snow White. Donald blushed with delight: for one dance, he would be Prince Charming!

Clarabelle and Goofy preferred the tango. To the sound of Dopey's accordion, they paced the floor and twirled and paced the floor again. When the dance was over, they received a hearty applause.

Huey, Dewey, and Louie were a little too young to enjoy the tango, so while Clarabelle and Goofy stole the show, they slipped down to the basement.

"Over there!" said Louie, pointing to an electrical box on the wall. He climbed on top of Dewey and opened it. They started to giggle. With one flick of the switch, everyone upstairs would be in the dark!

When the lights went off, Donald was so surprised
he did not know what to say. He had no time to scold
his three nephews because the instant they returned to
the room the show began!

"Take your seats!" giggled Dewey. "It's show time!"

"Pluto!" shouted the audience when the brave dog appeared on the screen. He was peacefully sleeping, but a slow and suspenseful music foretold a future mishap....

A crow stood in front of
Pluto and yelled at the top
of his lungs, "Wake up, you
lazy dog! Wake up! I dare
you to catch me!"

Pluto woke up with a
start. "Grrr..." he rumbled.

Pluto leapt up and the chase began! The audience was delighted. "Go, Pluto! Go!" they cheered.

Pluto went for the crow's tail. Just as he was about to catch it, the bird slipped into the house. Pluto followed him into the house while the audience laughed, "Faster! Faster!"

Inside the house, a big surprise awaited Pluto. Mickey was holding a huge birthday cake in his hands.

"Happy Birthday, Pluto!" sang his friends as he skidded to a stop.

"Don't look so surprised," teased Minnie. "Some crows are nice!"

Pluto thought it was kind of everyone to give him a cake, but it was really Donald's birthday.

"Yes, it is indeed Donald's birthday today!" said a voice from the back of the room. The lights were turned on.

"Gladstone Gander!" exclaimed Donald.

"In the flesh," said Gladstone, dressed to the hilt. He pointed to a huge present next to him and said, "My dear Donald, this is a very small gift for you. I hope it suits you."

"You hope it suits me?" asked Donald, not understanding.

"Yes, I hope it suits you, or pleases you, to put it plainly. In any case, I am sure that I am better at choosing gifts than our Uncle Scrooge!" he continued. "Just imagine, he gave me an hour glass for my birthday...."

Donald Duck and his friends listened carefully. They knew better than to interrupt Gladstone. Uncle Scrooge had meanwhile very quietly slipped under the table.

"An hour glass?" repeated Donald, not believing his ears.

"An hour glass!" insisted Gladstone. "An hour glass! Which furthermore wouldn't work, because the sand was so coarse it could not pass through the opening!"

"Hah! That little rascal!" said Donald with a chuckle.

"Indeed, he is a rascal!" continued Gladstone. "But I had my revenge! A week after he gave me this useless gift, I called him on the telephone. 'Hello, Uncle Scrooge!' I said. 'This is Gladstone calling to thank you for your marvelous gift! Since I've had it, my arthritis has disappeared; I won a whole new wardrobe; and my old aunt Adele died and left me a castle in Spain, a few summer houses by the sea and three million dollars! Your gift sure is a lucky charm, Uncle Scrooge! Thank you very much!' "

"The following day," Gladstone went on, "Uncle Scrooge came to see me. He wanted his gift back. He was even willing to part with a few of his beloved greenbacks!"

Gladstone started to laugh. "I gave him back the hour glass. The next day Uncle Scrooge called me. He was very upset: the night before he had been robbed! Tongue-in-cheek, I asked him, 'Did they leave the good luck charm behind?' 'That's all they left me!' cried Uncle Scrooge. 'I will get rid of it this very minute!' With that, he hung up on me!"

Just as Gladstone finished his story, the doorbell rang. Donald excused himself and went to open the door.

"Chip and Dale! How nice of you to remember my birthday," he said to his two friends at the door. "Come on in!"

"Look Uncle Scrooge! They found your stolen present!" said Donald as he read the calling card. "You did buy me a gift!"

Uncle Scrooge came out from under the table and blushed a deep red.

Donald opened the box and pulled out...the hour glass! Everyone in the room broke into laughter— everyone but Uncle Scrooge. "What is so funny?" he asked. But no one heard him. They were laughing too hard.

Donald called his friends to the dining room. Daisy had cooked a delicious meal!

After the dessert, he climbed on top of the table and announced, "My friends you have all been so good to me! Now please follow me to the garden where the grand finale awaits us!"

Everyone followed him outside. Donald stepped up to a detonator and said, "Now, stay still! And keep your eyes open, because you are about to see the greatest show ever!"

Donald pushed down the lever and *boom!* A million fireworks lit up the sky and trickled down as stars.

"Oooh! Aaah!" they gasped, all but one individual, who cried out for help.

"Goofy!" called Donald as his friend ran around the garden with his pants smoking. "Goofy! Sit on the wet grass!"

Goofy followed his friend's advice and sighed with relief.

The party came to an end and, though everyone was a little sad that the fun was over, they all had enjoyed themselves.

Even Goofy, who had lost his pants to the fireworks, was laughing.

"See you all next year!" he called out to Donald and his friends as he left.

Published by
Twin Books
15 Sherwood Place
Greenwich, CT 06830

ISBN 1-85469-966-0

Printed in Hong Kong

Reprinted 1992